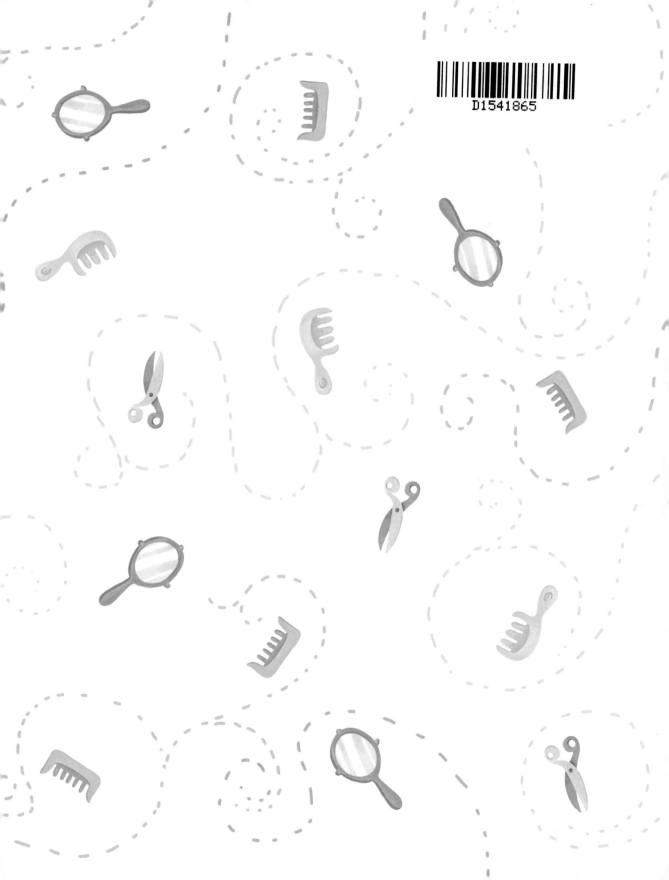

For my curly haired babies.
You are beautiful.
Love, Mama

First hardcover edition in this format 2021.

Summary: A celebration of diversity in children's hair.

Paperback ISBN: 979-8-9853318-1-3
Hardcover ISBN: 979-8-9853318-0-6
Ebook ISBN: 979-8-9853318-2-0
Printed in the United States of America
Set in Winter Mood with Semplicita Pro.
Edited by Emily Fuggetta. Illustrations and cover design by Alin Russ.

Special thanks to Dr. Temeka Brantley.

RC
&Me

All Hair Best

by
Elizabeth
Stoops

Big curls,
bigger
curls,

small curls,
tiny.

Straight hair,

straighter hair,

bright hair,

shiny.

Crew cut,
close-cropped, stiff hair, spikes.

Flat top, angled, tangled—yikes!

Thick hair, slick hair,
cut hair bangs.

Weave hair,
braid hair,
long hair hangs!

Kinky hair,
coiled hair, messy hair,
shag.

Shaved hair,
wavy hair, neat hair,
swag!

Ponytail, pigtails,
twists, and rows,

Bun hair, bob hair,
buzzed hair, bows.

Fluffy hair,

puffy hair,

ironed hair,

flat.

Wig hair, big hair, rainbow hair, hat!

Wash hair, dry hair,

sleepy hair
rests.

All hair happy.

All hair **BEST!**

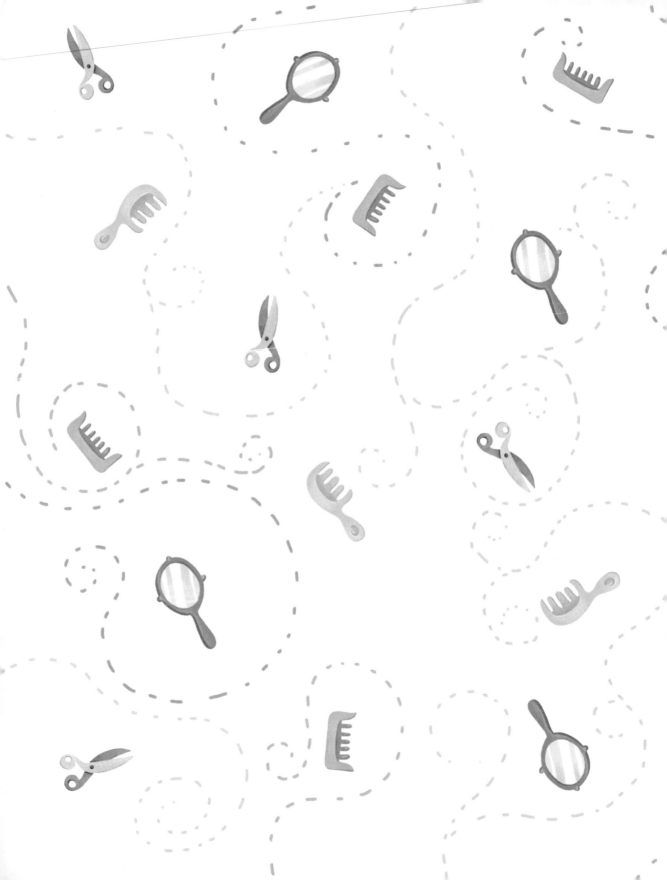

Made in the USA
Coppell, TX
27 April 2023

16126757R00017